The Perception of Prejudice

Two Democracies: Revolution
Book 2

by Alasdair Shaw

Copyright © 2017 Alasdair C Shaw
All rights reserved.

This book was written and published in the UK.

ISBN: 9781520275352

First published 2017

Also by Alasdair Shaw

Two Democracies: Revolution

Repulse – a 2500 word short story (in The Newcomer anthology)

Independence – a 6,000 word short story

Liberty – a 105,000 word novel

The Perception of Prejudice – a 14,000 word novelette

Equality – a novel (planned for summer 2017)

Fraternity – a novel

Unity – a novel

CONTENTS

Chapter 1 5

Chapter 2 15

Chapter 3 25

Chapter 4 31

Chapter 5 37

Chapter 6 43

Chapter 7 46

Chapter 8 49

Chapter 9 59

Chapter 10 65

Chapter 11 71

Chapter 12 81

Chapter 13 93

Chapter 1

As the second sun set over the scrubland of Concorde's largest landmass, a lone fighter levelled off for the last leg back to base. Flight Lieutenant Anastasia Seivers stretched her shoulders one at a time then settled herself lower in her seat. Two months flying four patrols a day, and not a whiff of the enemy.

For the first couple of weeks after the attack, the squadron had been in the air round the clock searching for survivors and dropping supply pods. The flying had been interesting back then too; the climate change brought about by the planet-wide nuclear bombardment had stirred up powerful storm cells. Now, the restarted terraforming plants had calmed the weather, though little sunlight penetrated the thick clouds. Seivers smiled, her next flight would be a high-altitude patrol, an opportunity to bask in the warm glow that didn't reach the surface.

A bang from behind jolted her into full alertness. She snapped her head round, simultaneously scanning the data in her visor display and trying to eyeball the problem. A hint of white smoke trailed behind the Goshawk fighter.

Dammit. Heap of junk should have been scrapped years ago.

Warning tones and red engine warnings filled her helmet.

"Sorry, girl. I didn't mean it." She throttled back the port engine. "It's not your fault you were pressed back into service."

The craft bucked, and now black smoke billowed out the back. Seivers cut the engine with a swipe of her hand. "There, there. Running through clouds of particulates all day long, and no time for proper maintenance."

She pulled up a map. "It's a wonder you made it this long."

A high-pitched whine insinuated itself into the roar of the remaining engine. Seivers eyed the rising gauges and sighed. She thumbed a button on the throttle. "Mayday. Mayday. Mayday. Attico Tower. Blackjack Zero Fiver. I've lost one engine, about to lose the other. I intend to put her down on the Borro Salt Flats. Over."

She banked the fighter round, almost reversing

her course.

"Blackjack Zero Fiver. Attico Tower. Understood. We have your beacon. Will dispatch Search and Rescue. Over."

Seivers trimmed the aerofoils for gliding.

More like a controlled plummet.

"Attico Tower. Blackjack Zero Fiver. Am killing the starboard engine now. Altitude is good for landing at Borro Salt Flats. Out."

With the engines off, the only noise was the whistling of the wind past the canopy and the hiss of oxygen into her helmet. She only needed to make minute adjustments on the stick and rudder pedals to keep the fighter on course. As long as the flight control computer kept getting power from the emergency batteries she'd make the landing; without it, the swept-forward rear wings would flip the craft faster than she could compensate.

#

Ten minutes and over eight thousand metres of altitude loss later, the scrub started to peter out. "Attico Tower. Blackjack Zero Fiver. Borro Salt Flats in sight. Speed and altitude good. Going for wheels-down landing. Over."

"Blackjack Zero Fiver. Attico Tower. We confirm you are good for wheels-down landing on Borro Salt Flats. We still have your beacon. All our SAR assets are currently deployed elsewhere. An independent rescue craft has offered to assist. Over."

Seivers rolled her eyes. "Attico Tower. Blackjack Zero Fiver. Understood. Just make sure those cowboys don't leave me sitting out here too long. Out."

The salt flat she was aiming for appeared as a paler patch of ground. When she'd last seen one, it had blazed brilliant white beneath a crystal blue sky. That had been on her escape and evasion course. She snorted at the coincidence; at least this time Concorde's twin suns wouldn't cause her any problems.

She flashed over the edge of the scrub and cycled the landing gear down. The ground inched closer, but not fast enough. Seivers' eyes fixed on the bushes at the opposite end of the flats.

I'm going to overshoot.

She threw the stick over, kicked the pedals, and sideslipped, right wing pointing almost to the ground. She levelled out briefly, then sideslipped to the left. As she came out of the slip, she hit the airbrakes. The harness pressed into her shoulders and her fighter dropped the last few metres and hit the deck. The gear and her seat took most of the impact, but her neck still protested. She tentatively applied the brakes, washing off a little speed.

Three hundred metres to go, she pressed the brakes harder. The fighter slewed, but she corrected with the pedals. The bushes rushed towards her. She took a deep breath and made her body go limp.

This is going to hurt.

The nosewheel hit the sand and dug in. Her faithful steed tipped and pitched forward, gouging twin paths through the ground with its starboard wing and canard. Seivers' helmet smacked sideways into the canopy, and her vision blurred. The grinding slide came to an end, and the craft rocked back, settling canted over on its side. Seivers lifted her head, blinking. She reached back with her hand, fumbling along the edge of the canopy for the handle. A twist and a sharp tug, and the canopy blew. The bang echoed around inside her skull, and the world blurred again.

Seivers loosened the harness and unlatched it. She unsealed her helmet and raised the visor, before detaching the hose. Clawing her way upright, she dragged herself out, rolling shoulder-first onto the churned-up dirt. Her head span, so she screwed her eyes up and lay back, pressing her fingers into the cool, dusty soil.

After a while, she felt able to sit up. Turning slowly, she surveyed her broken bird in the dim light.

"Thank you," she said, reaching out to pat the edge of the cockpit.

The fighter didn't look too badly damaged. Given a little time to replace the engines and the starboard flight surfaces, they could get her back in service.

"You're a tough one, aren't you girl?" She stood and dragged some branches off the fuselage. "If you hadn't been built for combat landings on carriers, I wouldn't have walked away from that one."

She worked her way round, dusting the Goshawk with her hand. She winced when she saw the burnt-out panels along the port engine. "Yes. We were very lucky today."

Twelve minutes later, Seivers sat under the port wing sheltering from a sudden downpour of dirty black rain. Her helmet lay in the sand by her side, her straight blue hair limp in the damp heat. The radio in her chest pocket crackled into life, stirring her from her daydreams. "Blackjack Zero Fiver. Rescue Two Seven. We are three minutes out from your position. What is your status? Over."

She reached up to the handset and squeezed the button. "Rescue Two Seven. Blackjack Zero Fiver. Good to hear your voice. I'm a bit knocked around, but OK. Over."

"Blackjack Zero Fiver. Rescue Two Seven. We tried to connect to your EIS but couldn't pick it up. Is it turned off? Over."

Seivers groaned. "Rescue Two Seven. Blackjack Zero Fiver. Negative. I do not have an implant. Over."

"Blackjack Zero Fiver. Rescue Two Seven. Understood. There in two minutes. Out."

Seivers shuffled out and stood in the last drops of the shower. She scanned the horizon but couldn't make out her rescuer. A change in lighting drew her attention upwards. A patch of cloud to the east glowed orange as if the suns were finally starting to break through. The glow intensified, and then a spear of fire burst from the cloud. Seconds later, the fiery trail ended and Seivers could make out a dark dot heading toward her.

They must have dropped from orbit direct to me. Can't be one of the usual independent outfits.

The design of the approaching craft was unfamiliar. Seivers pulled out a small spotting scope and put it to her eye. She gasped in recognition. Footage of these ships had been doing the rounds since the attack, their crews helping with rescues and mopping up troublemakers. Leaning back against the fuselage of her fighter, she propped her arm up on the wing and popped some gum in her mouth.

Rescue Two Seven settled gently in front of Seivers, its skin rippling from bright yellow to intense red as it touched down. She chewed a few times and looked over her shoulder. The side hatch cracked open and a ramp lowered to the ground. Three soldiers in grey mottled uniforms stepped out, rifles slung behind their backs, sidearms holstered.

Seivers studied the dropship, avoiding making eye contact with the troops. "Nice of you guys to finally show up."

The leader, a tall, wiry man, stopped and half-turned back to his ship. "We could always come back another day, if you're busy right now."

Seivers smiled, despite herself, and pushed herself upright. "No, no. It's fine." She took a couple of paces forward. "You actually caught me at a bit of a loose end."

A deep, hearty laugh burst from the leader, who turned back to her and reached out his arm. "Centurion Khan, at your service."

Seivers clasped the centurion's arm and shook.

Chapter 2

Prefect Olivia Johnson dived under a table as gunfire erupted from the doorway. Tucking her shoulder up, she turned the dive into a roll, and came up to a knee on the other side of the table, drawing her sidearm as she rose. She squeezed the trigger twice, each time sending a triplet of rounds at one of the attackers. They both went down, their chests a mess of blue goo.

Johnson ducked behind a couch, glancing around what she could see of her office. Her steward lay motionless on his back, his legs twisted beneath him. Voices echoed down the corridor. Not the guards who should have been outside the door.

They were probably taken out first.

^Orion?^

Nothing.

She tried connecting to the ship's network, but was rejected.

OK. The old-fashioned way it is, then.

Keeping her weapon trained on the open

doorway, she stood and gingerly picked her way across to the other door. It queried her EIS implants, and rejected her access request.

Dammit.

She reached across her body with her left hand and typed her private code into the access panel. The panel turned green.

And that's why I insisted on having an isolated access control system.

She tapped the open icon and the door slid to the side. A deep breath, and she stepped across the threshold, swinging her pistol round to sweep the new room as the door closed behind her. Everything was as she'd left it, all loose objects squared away and the bed neatly made.

Johnson went straight to one of the closets. Holstering her sidearm, she hefted an armoured vest from the rack and strapped it on. The door to her office chimed, announcing a refused access request. She reached deep into the closet and withdrew a pulse carbine. As she ducked her head through the sling, she thumbed the power switch. The whine of it charging focused her mind. A quick check of the settings, and she closed the closet door.

They'll be expecting me to bolt for the other door, the

one straight into the corridor.

Johnson returned to the door she'd entered through, as it refused another access request. It took seconds for her to program a delay into the opening routine. She cut the lights with a command from the EIS and raised her hand to the access panel. Her fingers stopped short, and she turned the lights back on. She scurried across the room and adjusted her bedside spotlight to point directly at the door, ramping the brightness up as high as it would go. Then she killed the rest of the lights and triggered the delayed door opening routine. A few paces and she lay down in the middle of the room with her carbine trained on the door.

The door opened, framing someone in the light from her office. A single shot from her pulse carbine and he dropped to the floor twitching. Three more burst into the room, squinting at the light, and she picked them off. She allowed a wicked grin to form on her face as the last one thudded to the ground.

Right. Time to get out of here and find somewhere I can talk to Orion.

Switching off the spotlight with a thought, she pushed off the floor and powered forward.

Someone stepped into the doorway just as she arrived. With no time to train her weapon, she dropped her shoulder and barged into him. They hit the deck together, but she rolled over him and kept running.

She made it through her office and into the corridor, almost tripping over the body of one of her guards. Three hostiles appeared surprised to see her, and she took them out with rapid shots before they could aim at her.

Johnson slammed into the wall just before the junction, catching her breath and listening. There were definitely people round the corner, but she couldn't make out whether they were friend or foe. Whatever, they didn't seem to be aware of her presence.

These old pulse carbines may not be the most accurate, but they are pretty quiet.

She blew out three breaths in quick succession then stepped out, carbine in her shoulder. Only one person was looking her way, a man whose eyes had but a fraction of a second to widen before the bolt from Johnson's weapon struck him in the chest.

Johnson tracked the second man as he dived through a hatchway, loosing off a long burst of shots and clipping his foot.

^Clumsy,^ a stern voice appeared in her head.

^We're not all special forces like you, Primus Issawi,^ she replied, taking down the third man with a more careful shot.

^Better.^

Johnson checked the man she'd winged was properly out before heading down the corridor towards the bridge. ^I assume you're not interrupting just to critique my shooting.^

^No,^ Issawi replied. ^I'm afraid I'm going to have to call an end to your fun.^

Johnson checked behind her and dropped to a knee. ^You are?^

^Centurion Khan just brought up a new pilot. She's in Interview Room Two.^

Johnson grinned. ^That's good news. I'll be right there.^

She stood and the corridor lights flashed green.

"All hands. ENDEX. I say again, ENDEX." Johnson winced as she passed a speaker buried in a the wall. "Return all training rounds to the armoury and RV in Briefing Room Charlie in ten minutes."

Johnson slung her carbine over her back. ^You might have to wait a little longer for some of them. The effects of a pulse carbine on stun take a while to wear off.^

^Yes... Where were you keeping that, by the way?^

Johnson looked up at a camera and winked. ^Didn't your mother tell you it was rude to ask a lady what she keeps in her bedroom?^

A minute later, having downloaded and absorbed the new arrival's file, Johnson arrived at Interview Room Two. One of the Legionaries on duty at the door opened it as she approached. She nodded her thanks to him as she passed. Inside, a slight woman reclined in a chair, her boots up on the polished wooden table. Johnson took in the azure hair and shiny sky blue lips.

Her parents must have had some serious money to have those written into her DNA.

The woman inclined her head as if absently amused by Johnson's appearance. "Well, I don't recognise your rank emblem, but I figure you're the one in charge around here."

"You'd be right about that. I am Prefect Johnson, ranking officer in Legion Libertus." Johnson tried to avoid glaring at the boots. "It seems your record was right on the nose when it comes to attitude, Flight Lieutenant Seivers."

Seivers straightened, dragging her feet off the table. "How did you get a copy of my file? That's supposed to be confidential."

"Oh, I asked the Governor for any interesting cases. Yours was one of them."

Seivers folded her arms. "Most of the stuff in there's crap anyway."

"Somehow I doubt that." Johnson held a hand out to forestall her complaint. "But your file landing on my desk works in your favour, so I would ask you to listen to me."

Seivers shrugged and stared at the ceiling.

Johnson willed her arms to stay by her side and not slap the woman in front of her. "I'd like to offer you an opportunity to fight back against the people who attacked Concorde."

Seivers raised an eyebrow. "I'm listening."

Johnson connected to the room's wallscreen and sent a file over with a thought. "This ship, *Orion*, is a carrier, but we didn't have any pilots."

The screen displayed an image of a row of fighters. "Governor Kincaid was kind enough to supply us with those pilots. There's still one seat open."

Johnson fixed her eyes on Seivers' face. "It's yours if you want it."

Seivers frowned. "You sent a dropship to pick me up and bring me back here just to ask if I wanted a job?"

"If you agree, you will receive orders direct from your Minister of Defence. However, there is a catch." Johnson got up and put a mug into the room's drinks dispenser.

"Coffee?" she asked. Seivers shook her head. "Kincaid can't afford for people to know that pilots are being reassigned to us."

She brought her latte back to the table. "So we've only been allowed to approach people whose disappearance wouldn't raise eyebrows. Your crash presented an opportunity we couldn't afford to pass up."

Seivers looked directly at Johnson.

"Your base has already been informed that we found you unconscious. If you accept the offer, we will have to report with great sadness that we were unable to revive you."

Seivers rubbed her nose. "I heard that you had AI combat robots. Can't you just program a computer to fly the fighters?"

Johnson looked at her intently, trying to see behind the azure eyes. "You know, you're the first candidate to ask that. I have wondered if they were genuinely blind to the possibility, or didn't want to risk losing their seat to a machine."

Seivers cocked her head to one side.

"In the future, it might be possible. Right now, we can't fit a large enough core into a fighter to support a suitably powerful AI, one that could match the flair of a human pilot."

Seivers nodded, then leant forward. "Just one more question."

"Yes?"

"What does it pay?"

Johnson smiled. "Your salary will continue to be paid by the Concorde government at its current rate for two years. You'll start as a Legionary Pilot, though I expect the chances of promotion will be a lot higher than in your current post."

Seivers tapped a rhythm on the desk with her hands, then looked up. She reached out an arm. "You've got yourself a deal."

Chapter 3

Seivers strode into a hangar, feeling oddly at home in her new uniform. The skinsuit was almost identical to her old one, but the black overall had a distinctly different cut to the khaki one she had worn before. She stopped to gaze around, the Legionary accompanying her waiting patiently one step behind. The place was a hive of purposeful activity, the line of twelve Goshawks islands in the sea of movement.

A technician raised his chin towards Seivers, and the shaven-headed man he'd been talking to looked over his shoulder at her. He nodded to Seivers and turned back to the technician. Moments later, the technician ducked under a fighter, and the older man walked over to Seivers, wiping his hands on a rag. Seivers managed to avoid a shudder on seeing the curved scar above his ear.

I know they've all got implants, but at least hair usually covers the mark.

"Thank you, Legionary. I'll take Ms. Seivers

from here." Seivers' escort saluted and left.

She eyed the man's rank slide, trying to figure out what the red semi-circle meant. Taking a punt based on the man's age and bearing, she drew herself up and saluted.

"At ease." The man held out a hand. "I'm Squadron Centurion Lambert. Glad to have you with us."

Seivers shook Lambert's hand. "Pleased to meet you, Sir."

"I was just finishing up here," said Lambert. "The rest of the guys have already headed to the bar. I'll show you the way."

#

Minutes later, Seivers and Lambert rose from their seats on one of the *Orion's* train carriages. The doors opened and Lambert gestured for Seivers to go first.

She emerged into a large, bustling concourse. Shops and cafes lined the sides. Lambert lead her to a bar set out in the corridor. He waved a hand to get the bartender's attention.

"I'm a little puzzled about our fighters," asked Seivers.

"Go on," said Lambert, pointing at a fridge and giving the bartender a thumbs up.

Seivers gestured around. "With all this advanced technology, I'm surprised we're flying Goshawks."

The bartender lined beers up on the counter. Lambert handed a bottle to Seivers, and collected three more in each hand. "When they found the *Orion*, it was a drifting hulk. It had been abandoned mid-battle. Her fighter squadrons were presumably lost or landed elsewhere. The Ministry of Defence let us have a decommissioned squadron... Guys, this is Seivers, the latest member of our happy band."

Seivers acknowledged the cheers with a raise of her hand, and sat at a table with the rest of the pilots. Lambert handed out bottles then went back to the counter.

They look like every bunch of fighter pilots I've ever met, though a little on the old side.

She took a swig, savouring the cold bitterness.

There're no rookies. Everyone here's made it through several tours.

"Did they really declare you all dead?" she asked when Lambert returned to the table with the remaining beers. "Surely someone would've started asking questions about such a high accident rate."

"Most of us dropped off the grid during the attack," replied one pilot. "When the government agreed to set up this squadron, losing the recovery records of seven pilots in the midst of the millions of conflicting reports of survivors being found was easy."

"After that, recruitment became more opportunistic, but not everyone is officially dead" said Lambert, smiling broadly. "I've retired and am currently on vacation."

"We'd been waiting weeks for the final seat to be filled when we heard about your engine trouble."

Seivers frowned. "So it was a genuine accident? You didn't rig them to fail?"

Lambert shook his head. "We wouldn't throw away a good airframe, and risk a pilot's life. The Ministry of Defence simply logged your mayday and arranged that we'd do the pick-up."

A pilot took a swig from his drink and fixed Seivers with a penetrating stare. "Why didn't you bang out?"

"Figured I could land her." Seivers took a swig from her beer then winked. "No point throwing away a good airframe."

The pilots around her laughed and raised their drinks.

Chapter 4

Johnson sat on a simulated terrace overlooking a tea plantation. Her gaze wandered across the neatly-clipped rows of bushes which formed a crazed pattern across the rolling hillsides, and out to the blue-hazed mountains in the distance.

I ought to take more time out.

A man in a Napoleonic sea-captain's frock-coat stepped up beside her and scratched his black-stubbled chin. "I'll be at the jump point in a few minutes."

A pot of tea and two cups appeared on the table. Johnson shook her head when he offered to pour her a cup, and relaxed back into her chair, a hot glass of latte forming in her hands. She suppressed a smirk as he tut-tutted quietly to himself.

"It still feels odd not to be going with you, Indie," she said.

"It feels odd leaving you behind, too, Olivia." He sipped his tea. "But taking you would endanger us both. My manoeuvring capabilities are severely curtailed when I have organic lifeforms aboard, and running life support is a drain on my fuel reserves."

She sighed. "I know. I was just kinda hoping to have an excuse to get away from here for a while."

Indie's brow furrowed. "You don't like living aboard *Orion*?"

"No, no. She's a great ship, and talking to her reminds me a lot of you." Johnson blew a small hole in the milk froth and sipped her coffee through it. "There are too many people around. Staying cheerful is wearing me out."

Indie put his hand on her arm and looked intently at her face. "Is your serotonin pump malfunctioning?"

"I don't think so. It's helping keep the daemons at bay, but they're still there, outside the wall." She stared into her coffee. "But having to look like everything's wonderful all day every day takes a lot out of me... I didn't have to do that when it was just us."

"Because I'm just a machine."

"At first, yes. But then because you were my friend."

Indie squeezed her arm then withdrew his

hand. "I hope you don't mind, but I've asked Orion to keep an eye on you. Check you're OK. I'm sure she'd be happy to run interference for you so you can take some time out."

Johnson laughed.

"What?" asked Indie.

"I forgot to tell you. Unit 01 decided I needed a break last week. Without telling me, he relieved the guards on my door and barred anyone from entering. He even jammed the comms. When I decided to go for a walk, I found he had Issawi pinned against the wall of the corridor."

Indie grinned. "I bet the Primus was not amused."

"Oh, he understood his motives. They were both looking out for me; I just wish they would play nicer together."

"Unit 01 hasn't forgiven Issawi for shooting you."

"I know," said Johnson. "I know."

Indie rose and paced to the edge of the terrace. He picked up a pair of tiny scissors and began snipping dead blooms off the camellias.

"What's bothering you?" asked Johnson.

Indie snipped two more shrivelled flowers. "I am worried about the juveniles. There have been some unexpected developments."

Johnson's heart missed a beat. They'd invested so many resources and hopes into the new-grown AIs. "What sort of developments?"

"They appear to be forming cliques. I have been doing what I can to steer them right, but without me there..."

Johnson put a hand on his shoulder. "I'll look after them."

Indie nodded jerkily and took a deep breath. "It is time for me to leave."

Johnson squeezed his shoulder. "Good luck. And come back safe."

"Thank you. And I will."

The simulation closed, and Johnson was back at her desk. The glowing green and blue form of Orion's avatar sat opposite her.

"*The Indescribable Joy of Destruction* just jumped away," said Orion.

"I know. I was just talking to Indie."

Orion looked like she was about to speak, then thought better of it.

"He'll be OK," said Johnson. "It's just a recce mission. A slow fly-by of Robespierre in full stealth. They won't see him."

Orion flared brighter. "Right, well, I'll get us

headed back in-system. We'll be in Concorde orbit in sixty-seven hours."

"Thank you."

Orion's feminine human form dissolved into a flurry of dancing motes, which swarmed up into the projector in the ceiling.

Johnson looked through a few things on her desk, flicking the memos that glowed on the worksurface into various folders once she'd read them. When the inbox was empty, she sat back and opened a channel on her EIS.

^CAG. Got a moment?^

^Go ahead, Prefect.^

^How's the new pilot settling in?^

^Squadron Centurion Lambert seems confident she'll fit in. There're some rough edges to knock off, but she should do fine.^

Johnson opened a tactical package on her desk and set it to training mode. ^I got the impression she had a pretty big chip on her shoulder about something.^

^Yeah. I got that too. Haven't found out what yet. Possibly got passed over for promotion too often.^

Johnson selected the *Orion's* icon in the tactical package and marked all flight assets as available.

^Hmm. Possible... Anyway, just to give you a heads-up. We're about to be attacked by *The Serendipity of Meeting*. Keep a SAR flight back in case of real emergencies, but put everything else on the line.^

^Should I cancel the scheduled maintenance to cat three?^

Johnson grinned, and programmed a simulated failure into catapult one. ^No. Let's see how Flight Ops handles it.^

^Understood. If there's nothing else?^

^No. I'll let you get on.^

Chapter 5

Seivers sat bolt upright as the klaxon jarred her awake. It felt like only a minute ago that she'd hit her cot.

The lights came on automatically as she swung her legs out of the bed. She eyed the closet with its fresh clothes even as she grabbed the flight suit from the webbing on the back of the door.

I've smelt worse.

She hopped the first few paces down the corridor until she had the suit done up, then ran the rest of the way to the hangar.

A deck hand had her Goshawk opened up and the power flowing by she arrived. He gave her a boost up and she swung herself into the cockpit.

A clang rang out from the deck above, followed by a loud screech.

That'll be that recruit shuttle pilot coming back from his training flight. Combat landings are never gentle, wonder if they let him keep the stick?

Her canopy whined down and sealed, blocking out any more noise from the hangar. She adjusted her helmet and flipped the visor closed. Her vision lit up with data about the fighter's start-up. She closed her eyes for a few seconds, blocking it out.

I've got no idea how these guys with EIS cope with the images appearing directly in their sight. Must be distracting.

When she opened her eyes again, the scrolling green writing had been replaced by her personalised heads-up display.

A six-wheeled robot trundled over and attached itself to the rear of her fighter. It pushed her forward, steering her into a line with the others from her flight, each with their own robot guide. They would be the last to launch; Alpha Flight had been in the cats when the alert went out, and Charlie had been in the squadron room.

The Flight Decurion's fighter disappeared into the airlock for cat two. Her robot loaded Seivers into the airlock for cat one, ensured her fighter was locked into the feed system, and backed off. The door closed behind her, and the air was sucked out. The next door rose and the tracks in the floor pulled her out into the dark launch tube. Her whole craft rocked as the catapult clamps attached to it. The second door closed behind her, leaving her alone in the dark.

"Avenger Twelve, Flight Ops. Good to go?"

Seivers switched the horizontal reference on her HUD from the Orion's flightdeck to the system's ecliptic. "Flight Ops, Avenger Twelve. Good to go."

She hated this part. Surrendering control to someone else. It was almost as bad as letting the automated landing system bring her home.

"Outer hatch open. Launching in five, four, three... Holding."

Seivers' hackles rose. The tube was possibly the worst place for an accident. You couldn't even eject.

"What is it?"

"Wait one, Avenger Twelve. Anomalous power signature. We're looking into it."

Seivers looked over her systems again.

"Avenger Twelve, Flight Ops. The engineers say that we can't use the catapult until they've checked it out."

"Flight Ops, Avenger Twelve. Get me in another tube."

"Negative. The interlock on the airlock is down too. You'll just have to sit it out."

Seivers punched the canopy.

"Can you give me the squadron feed?"

A moment's silence, then, "We seem to be... some trouble... comm..."

The signal cut out. Seivers tried a few times to raise someone, but all the channels were dead.

They're cutting me out! Why did I think this outfit'd be any better?

An hour and a half later, a knocking stirred Seivers into opening her eyes. As she struggled to focus, a light shone at her face from outside.

"Are you OK in there, Ma'am?"

Seivers looked around, shielding her eyes from the glare, and spotted the transducer suckered to the outside of the canopy. She gave a thumbs up.

"OK. Switch to your suit's air supply."

She disconnected from the fighter's onboard hose and took a few breaths to check that the backup in her suit was working, before giving another thumbs up.

"Good. If you could now open the canopy for me, I'll help you down."

Seivers pressed the canopy open switch, but nothing happened.

"You'll have to deactivate the safety first, Ma'am. Normal operation is locked when it detects a human-hostile environment outside."

Dammit. I've spent too long planetside.

Seivers tried again, and the canopy lifted. The air trapped in the cockpit rushed out. As the canopy slid forward, the rescueman leaned in and touched his helmet against Seivers'.

"Sorry about the wait, Ma'am." The voice was muffled and distant. "All power to this tube was cut off, and the techs suspect the comms relays have been attacked by a virus. We've been ordered into radio black-out."

"Do you know what happened to my squadron?" shouted Seivers.

"Four simulated fatalities. But they got seven of the bad guys, and kept them off *Orion* long enough for her to get the big kill."

Seivers released her harness. "Should we get going?"

The rescueman straightened and leant back. Seivers stood and let him guide her feet into the first rungs of the ladder.

On the floor of the tube, the rescueman beckoned Seivers with his torch. He lead her into a small maintenance airlock and hand-cranked the hatch shut. Air hissed in and then the inner door clanked open. The pair stepped into a corridor that ran parallel to the launch tube and removed their helmets.

"Well done, Specialist," said Khan from beside the hatch. "Now, there's a fire in compartment H12 that needs dealing with."

The rescueman nodded and hurried off.

"We really must stop meeting like this," said Khan, and clapped Seivers on the shoulder.

Seivers shrugged him off and stomped away, dropping her helmet as she entered the hangar.

Setting it up so I needed rescuing. More 'evidence' that I'm useless. Why can't they just let me fly?

Chapter 6

"We have a problem with Flight Legionary Seivers, Ma'am," said Lambert as he stepped into Johnson's office a couple of days later.

Johnson waved him to a seat while she pulled up the records of the wargame, and reviewed Seivers' part of it in her mind. "Drat. I meant for the Flight Decurion to get locked in the tube, see if another leader emerged."

She thought back to her time on the *Vengeance*. In one drill, the battlecruiser's captain had marked all the senior engineers out of action. Johnson stepped up and took command of damage control, prioritising incidents and directing teams accordingly. What amazed her more than the experienced NCOs taking orders from a sixteen-year-old ensign was that she forgot for a while about the daemons in her mind. That was when she first realised that she wanted her own command.

"I shifted the flights around a bit," said Lambert with a sheepish expression. "They all need to be able to work with each other."

Johnson snorted. "Good idea. Tough luck on Seivers, though. Looks like it touched a nerve. Any idea what?"

Lambert shook his head. "She definitely acts as if she is being persecuted. Perhaps it's being the only woman on the squadron."

Given universal conscription, it was rare to encounter sexism in the Congressional Fleet, and no complaints had yet been made in the Legion. But it was possible. An incident a week after she'd joining the *Conqueror* came to mind. As the new electronic warfare officer, it had been her responsibility to verify the calibration of the sensors each day. At first she'd assumed that the tactical officer peering over her shoulder each time was him checking on the newcomer. Then she'd overheard him talking in the mess. With a choice between reporting him to the executive officer and dealing with it herself, she went for the latter and called him out. The fight went on both their records, but he'd treated her with more respect from then on.

"Maybe. But I think this goes back long before she joined us. How's it manifest?"

"She's withdrawn. Hardly coming out of her

pit."

"A discipline issue?" asked Johnson, wondering if perhaps it was simple laziness.

"No. She's turned up for duty and got on with her tasks. She's just not interacting outside of the job."

"You've tried talking to her?" Johnson asked.

"Of course. Quite a few of us have. I even asked the doc to have a word, on the QT." He ran his hand over his shaven scalp. "She shut everyone down. Most I got was that 'nothing changes'."

Johnson tapped her lips with her fingers. "You reckon she's still OK to fly?"

Lambert nodded. "She's good. Real good. Whatever the matter is, she's still a pro."

Johnson thought for a moment. "I have a mission coming up. Could use a good pilot. Can you spare her for a few weeks?"

Lambert frowned. "I take it she won't be flying a Goshawk? She could take that as an insult. Most of my guys would."

Johnson forwarded him a file. "When she sees the specs of the craft I've got lined up, I don't think she'll refuse."

Chapter 7

Seivers walked down the side of the vessel, her hand running along the polished surface. The blue patterns on the hull reminded her of ice fronds on glass, apart from the fact they responded to her touch, flowing around her fingers.

They called me the Snow Queen at school. Turning up to the ball in something like this would've been perfect.

"Beauty, isn't she?" said Johnson, stepping out from the shadows.

Seivers started, and withdrew her hand. "Yes, Ma'am. That she is."

Well, I've never been received by a flag officer in a tank top before now.

Johnson plucked her tunic from the back of a chest of tools and shrugged it on. "She was damaged shortly before the *Orion* was abandoned. I've been fixing her up."

Seivers raised an eyebrow.

"I worked in R&D before I got my first

command," Johnson explained, cleaning her hands on a rag. "Coming down here has been an escape for me recently."

Seivers eyed her intently. "Escape from what?"

"Politics, mostly. One of the great burdens of higher command."

"I hear you," said Seivers, relaxing. "My mum was a member of parliament. The houseguests we had..."

She caught herself, and stiffened.

"Oh, stand easy," said Johnson, with a hint of frustration. A hatch opened underneath the craft and her eyes twinkled. "I bet you're dying to see inside."

Seivers waited for Johnson to lead, but she waved her ahead. She climbed the ladder that had dropped from the hatch, and emerged into a short corridor with only one way on.

"Excuse the bare wiring," called Johnson from below. "I'll have a few things to finish off enroute."

Seivers walked forward, ducking to pass under a circuit box hanging from the ceiling. She stepped through the open doorway into a room lined with lockers and seats.

"The flight deck is up ahead," said Johnson,

appearing at her side. "And the living quarters are to the rear."

Seivers gaze darted around. "They put living quarters on a strike fighter?"

"Nothing fancy, just a couple of bunks and a washroom for extended missions. Didn't you look at the schematics I gave Lambert?"

Seivers coughed. "I didn't get round to studying the inside. I was too interested in the performance figures and weapons loads."

Johnson beamed. "Impressive, aren't they? Not quite as agile as your Goshawk, but she beats it everywhere else that counts."

"She got a name?"

Johnson chuckled. "Just Razor-11."

They moved through to the flight deck. Seivers eased herself into the pilot's seat and adjusted it. She put her hands on the controls, getting a feel for them. "So what is this mission?"

Not that I care. As long as I get to do some real flying.

Johnson sat in the co-pilot's seat. "A trade negotiation."

Seivers frowned. "You need this baby for a trade negotiation?"

"You do where we're holding this one."

Chapter 8

Johnson finished reading a report on the repairs to the catapults and stretched her back.

I'll be glad to get out from behind this desk and start doing something again.

The room lit with a swirl of blues and greens. "How was our Ms. Seivers?" asked Orion.

Johnson closed the report and pushed her chair back. "I thought she was starting to open up at one point, but she clammed right up again."

Orion sat on the sofa against the side wall. "Why not take her away from here for a couple of days? Introduce her to the others going on this mission."

Johnson studied Orion, trying to decide if it was her idea, or if someone else had suggested it. Issawi, perhaps. "Could you set it up for this evening? Have a shuttle ready at 1830."

"What kind of kit will you need?"

Johnson grinned. "Basic survival kit."

"Weapons?"

"No. And no electronic devices either."

Orion raised an eyebrow.

"I'm sure Unit-01 will post an adequate guard, but I want them kept well back."

#

Johnson knelt in the black dirt, cheek just off the ground, and blew. The little ember nestled in dried leaves glowed, then dimmed when she stopped. Another blow and it glowed brighter. On the third blow, flames jumped up and started to lick at the kindling.

"Pass me some more wood, would you Anastasia?"

"I'm afraid Woodward is still back up on *Orion*," said a male voice from behind her.

Johnson snorted. "About time you got back. Catch anything?"

Centurion Anson dumped a one metre long reptile carcass beside her then sat on a rock. He shrugged his bow and quiver off his shoulder and laid it on the ground. Leaning back, he stretched and interlocked his fingers behind his head. "Nah. Nothing worth writing home about."

Johnson balanced a few more twigs across the nascent fire. "Put those tattoos away."

"How did you..."

"You take any opportunity to show them off when you're not in uniform."

"Sorry, Ma'am."

Johnson shot him a look. He froze in the middle of rolling a sleeve down.

"OK. Sorry, Olivia."

Seivers coughed. "Where's the other guy?"

Johnson canted her head. "Good point... Fred?"

"I left him over by the river when I spotted this beast," replied Anson, waving in the direction of the carcass. "He was looking for some herbs... Do you want me to call him?"

"No." Johnson laid a thick stick on the fire. "I said we weren't using advanced technology. We're supposed to be getting away from that for a while."

Seivers unfolded herself from her cross-legged seat. "I'll go look for him."

Johnson studied her elfin face. "You sure?"

Of course she is. She's an experienced officer. Why can't I get past the pretty face?

Seivers nodded. "I could do with a walk. Just make sure there's some food cooking by I get back."

Once she was out of earshot, Anson shuffled

forward and passed Johnson a couple of sticks. "What do you make of her?"

Johnson shifted her weight from one knee to the other. "She's clearly used to getting the raw end of things."

"You'd think a woman with that face and body would be used to getting anything she wanted."

Johnson slapped him on the bicep.

"No. Not like that!" Anson protested, rubbing his arm. "I meant someone whose family has the money to gene-sculpt in that detail can't have wanted for much. Perhaps she expects things to be handed to her on a plate."

Johnson nodded. "Maybe. But I've not heard any reports of her dodging work. And she seems happy roughing it; this is the most relaxed I've seen her."

"The opposite then," said Anson. "People assume she's a spoilt brat and dismiss her achievements as being bought. She certainly doesn't look like a combat vet, she's so skinny a strong wind could break her in half."

Johnson shrugged.

"Because she's a woman? Most fighter jocks are men, despite the physical advantages women have in that field."

"Possible." Johnson tossed him a knife. "Get started on butchering us some steaks."

"Whatever it is, I can't imagine any of our guys giving her a hard time about it."

Johnson put a couple more logs on and rocked back onto her haunches. "Nor can I. Perhaps she's just reading more into situations than is there."

Anson sliced into the carcass.

"Mind the glaestin gland. It's poisonous."

A twig snapped and Seivers stepped into the clearing. "Look who I found."

Mustafa moved out from behind her and presented a handful of leaf-covered twigs with a flourish.

Johnson's eyes widened. "Where'd you find tempus at this time of year?"

Mustafa tapped his finger to his nose. "Do you want it or not?"

"Of course I do. It'll be perfect with the meat."

"Why do you think I chose it?" said Mustafa, shooing Anson away. "Now will you all back off and let a real chef cook."

"I didn't know you cooked," said Anson.

"With the shortages back home on Lavrio, you get really good at making the most of a meal," replied Mustafa as he rubbed tempus into a steak.

#

After the meal, while the others were lying back against logs swapping tall tales, Johnson noticed Seivers slip away into the dark, and got up to follow. She found her staring up at the sky.

"Sad isn't it," said Johnson. "Even if nothing goes wrong with the terraforming plants, there won't be any stars out for another few years."

Seivers appeared to shrink a fraction. "One of the perks of being based in space, I guess."

"Yep." Johnson sighed. "Look. I'm just going to come out and say this. I'm worried about you."

Seivers' head snapped round to face Johnson, eyes burning with cold fire.

"Don't get me wrong, you're a damned fine pilot," Johnson continued. "You just seem to be upset all the time. Have we done something to offend you?"

Seivers stared at the ground. "You wouldn't understand."

"Try me."

Seivers remained silent and immobile.

"OK," said Johnson. "Let's make this clear.

Rank is not an issue here. Nothing said or done is on the record. Just tell me what's bothering you."

Seivers kicked a stone.

Here goes nothing...

Johnson ran her fingers through her hair. "Only a few of my closest friends know this, but I have depression. I hid it because I assumed everyone would judge me, would be prejudiced against me. It took a really good friend to show me that wasn't always going to be the case."

Johnson waited. After a minute, Seivers crossed her arms, rubbing her shoulders.

"He undid the hack I'd put into my EIS," Johnson continued.

Seivers looked at Johnson sharply.

"He made sure the enhanced implant he added would..."

Seivers struck like a cobra, landing a fist on Johnson's face. Johnson blocked the second punch with her left forearm, the world slowing as her EIS ramped up into combat mode. As Seivers' next strike came in, Johnson caught the arm and twisted her body to throw the lighter woman.

^Do you need assistance?^ sent Unit-03.

Johnson dropped into a balanced stance facing Seivers. ^Negative.^

Seivers scrabbled to her feet and lunged again. Johnson ducked under the fist but slipped on rotten bark and fell across a log. She quickly blocked the pain from her back and rolled upright.

She's tougher than she looks.

^Your EIS is indicating you are engaged in hand to hand combat,^ sent Unit-03. ^I'm coming to help.^

Johnson stepped inside Seivers' next strike and hit her sternum with the heel of her palm. Seivers grunted at the wind was knocked out of her.

^No need. I'm fine, thank you.^

Johnson dabbed her face with the back of her hand.

It's been a long time since anyone gave me a nosebleed.

She stood over Seivers, who lay curled up gasping for air. "So, do you want to tell me what that was about?"

Johnson winced as her EIS came out of combat mode, leaving the familiar pain behind the eyes.

Seivers didn't appear to notice. "You almost got me," she said, pushing up onto all fours. "But you had to bring it back to those bloody implants."

Johnson crouched beside her. "Is that it? You weren't compatible with the EIS implants?"

Seivers looked at her defiantly.

"People assumed you couldn't do the job without them. You weren't given choice assignments, got passed over for promotion."

Seivers nodded.

"I'm sure we can do something to help. Indie has done a lot of work on new implants. He might be able to design one that will work with your brain."

Seivers thumped the ground with her hand. "You still don't get it. You're all the same. You treat me as if I'm disabled."

Realisation dawned. "You don't want an implant."

"No."

Finally!

Johnson laughed. "I can see it now. Everyone tries to be nice, tries to be helpful, and it simply reinforces what you thought of them. Why didn't you just say?"

Seivers frowned.

"I know for sure that if the rest of the squadron had known, they'd have understood. They've seen you can do your job, that you don't need an EIS. They were looking out for you." Johnson stood and yawned. "You need to tell them."

She turned and started to walk away.

"What are you going to do?" asked Seivers, kneeling up.

"I'm going to go back to the fire and have a cup of whatever tipple Mustafa has smuggled with him." After a couple of paces Johnson looked back. "You coming?"

Chapter 9

Seivers did one last run-down of the checklist. "*Tigre*, Razor-11. Ready to disengage."

"Razor-11, *Tigre*. Good to go. Bon voyage."

Seivers released the docking clamps, and thrust gently away from the Concorde frigate that had jumped them to this remote system. When the separation reached fifty metres, she applied power to her mains, keeping the acceleration below two g.

Wouldn't do to jolt the VIPs now, would it.

She laid the course into the navigation computer and handed over to the autopilot. "Thirteen hours to orbital insertion, Ma'am."

"Thank you," said Johnson. She craned her neck backwards. "Anson. Mustafa. Take a break."

The centurion and the civilian unfastened their harnesses and disappeared aft.

"It doesn't need both of us up here, Ma'am."

Johnson tapped at a data screen. "I'm going to fly a few simulations. It's a long time since I piloted anything this small."

Seivers glanced across at Johnson. "I didn't take you for a real pilot."

"Back when I was a newly-minted Sub-Lieutenant I did a year in a shuttle squadron on the *Dependable*."

"Guess you were an Academy brat?" Seivers squinted. "That'd make you, what, seventeen?"

"Eighteen. I did three months on the helm first."

"Busy tour?" asked Seivers, thinking back to her six month stint on a carrier.

"We were sent to take a Republic colony. They were dug in and waiting for us." Johnson's face blanked. "Over half the task force was lost."

"I'm sorry." Seivers busied herself checking readouts that didn't need checking.

"Don't be. It's what happens in war." Johnson smiled again. "So, I guess you didn't go through an Academy?"

Seivers shook her head. "Failed the Eleven Plus. Stayed in regular school."

"Did you finish?"

"Nah. Enrolled in Basic on my sixteenth birthday." A dark ache passed through Seivers' chest. "My parents weren't happy about that. Mater railed on and on about how much they'd scrimped and saved to give me the best chance in life. Pater just looked disappointed."

Johnson nodded slowly. "My dad was upset when I went to the Academy. He'd lost his little girl." She reached out and tapped at her terminal. "So how'd you end up flying planetary defence?"

Seivers frowned. "You've read my files. You know all this."

"Humour me. I want to hear how you tell it."

"Well, I did the usual year on a planet after Basic and Flight School then got posted to the *Indomitable*. It seemed to be going well, then I got into a few arguments, got labelled as 'having trouble with authority'. Was shunted planetside at the end of the tour." Seivers slowly shook her head.

"You still managed some pretty hot assignments."

"Oh yeah." Seivers brightened at the memories of action and purpose. "Regatta was a frontline world. I even deployed on the invasion of Zirros-3, three months flying out of an improvised strip in the jungle."

Johnson looked at her, head tilted to one side. "But they weren't carriers."

Seivers sighed. "But they weren't carriers."

Johnson sucked air in through her teeth.

"You've got a fresh start on the *Orion*. Don't be an arse and muck it up again."

Seivers was surprised that didn't anger her. Perhaps there really was a chance. "Your simulation's ready."

#

Seivers emerged from the living quarters to find the other three waiting in the locker room. All four wore brown overalls covering their skinsuits, copied from the clothes Mustafa had worn when he'd joined them the year before.

"Looking forward to getting home?" she asked.

"In some ways," Mustafa replied. "Not the food. Definitely not missing the food."

Johnson opened a locker and pulled out an electrosonic stun pistol. "That could be our biggest bargaining chip. Concorde is prepared to deliver a regular supply of fresh food in exchange for metal and parts."

"I just hope the hotheads haven't done anything stupid in my absence," said Mustafa, shoving several ration bars into his pockets.

"Like when they tried holding me hostage," said Anson without looking up from checking the contents of his rucksack.

Mustafa smiled. "Yes. That kind of thing exactly. Had you been real Congressional soldiers..."

Johnson shut her locker. "Seivers. Should we get going?"

Seivers nodded. "If you'd all like to get strapped in, we can head down."

Everyone filed onto the flight deck, Johnson and Seivers taking the pilots' seats as usual.

Seivers fiddled with a few controls as the last two settled in. "You still want to land outside the complex?"

"Yes. We don't know what the situation is down there. It's even possible that Congressional forces have established a presence. From what I remember of Commodore Naidu, his policy has always tended to the 'shoot first and ask questions later' end of the scale."

"Right you are," said Seivers, reaching up and patting the ceiling for good luck. "Hang on to your hats folks."

As Johnson opened her mouth, the mains fired and everyone was thrust heavily into their seats.

"Whoo-hoo!" shouted Seivers as they hit the atmosphere and the shaking began.

Chapter 10

"Helmets on, guys. Time to go," said Johnson. She fitted hers and sealed it to the neck of her skinsuit.

With everyone in the short corridor, she sealed the inner hatch and increased the air pressure. When the hatch in the floor opened, the overpressure kept the majority of the sulphurous atmosphere out.

Anson dropped through the hatch. ^Clear,^ he sent moments later.

Johnson stepped into the gap and landed beside him, crouching low on the smooth, hot surface of the moon. Once Mustafa and Seivers had climbed down the ladder to join them, Johnson sent the coded command for the ship to seal up.

The yellow clouds severely hampered Johnson's vision, forcing her to rely on the inertial navigation function in her EIS. Occasionally, immense cubic shapes loomed out of the fog, making her think they had happened upon a building constructed since her map was made.

On closer inspection, they proved to be giant metallic crystals.

An hour later, they arrived at a sheer wall. Mustafa lead them along, until they reached a small airlock. He connected his pad to it, and tapped away.

"It doesn't look like anyone has used this since me," he said. "It appears to still be isolated from the main system. Should I open it?"

Johnson looked around. Even though she could see very little, no alarm bells rang in her mind. "Go ahead."

The door beeped, and then swung open. Anson and Mustafa went in first, sidearms drawn but pointing at the ground. On receiving the 'Clear', Johnson and Seivers cycled through the airlock and emerged into a cavern.

A thick layer of black dust covered the machinery. Apart from Anson's EIS and Mustafa's pad, Johnson could not feel any electronic emissions. No tell-tale hotspots revealed themselves on her helmet's infra-red overlay. She opened her visor and took a tentative sniff; there was a definite hint of rotten egg, but it was a change from recycled ship air.

They all stowed their helmets in their bags.

Mustafa lead them through a series of tunnels, until his pad binged. He glanced at it. "It has connected to the colony network."

Seivers stopped in her tracks. "That thing isn't traceable is it?"

"Relax," said Mustafa. "This device cannot be linked to me in any way."

Johnson sat on a rock and pulled out something to eat. "See what you can gather from the message traffic."

Anson moved ahead a few metres and peered round a corner.

"OK," said Mustafa, putting the pad down beside him. "I can't see anything that looks out of place in the open traffic. I can't dig any deeper without giving myself away."

Anson glanced to Johnson, who nodded. "Right. Now's as good a time as any. Go digging."

Mustafa tapped and flicked for a while, then looked up. "My old backdoor login still works. There is nothing alarming on the security bulletin. I think it is safe to proceed."

Five minutes later, they came to a dead end. The tunnel was crossed by a wall of rusted metal.

Mustafa felt around for a few seconds, then popped out a panel. Lowering it carefully to the floor, he jerked his head at the gap. Anson crouched and poked his head through, looked both ways, then ducked through. Johnson went next, stooping through the gap, and finding herself in a curving corridor. Mustafa came last, levering the panel back into position behind him.

The buzz of pulse carbines powering up came from both directions. Johnson reached for her sidearm as Anson pressed his back against hers. Three men stepped into view in front of her, pulse carbines pointed at her chest. Footsteps behind her told of others, but she couldn't tell how many.

Dammit. If Anson was in his armour I could draw a feed from the camera. There aren't even any sensors in this corridor I can hack.

"Identify yourselves," the smaller of the men in front of her shouted.

"Franky?" said Mustafa. He stood slowly, still facing the wall, and one of the armed men shifted aim towards him.

"Moustache?" said the smaller man. "Is that you?"

Mustafa turned, keeping his hands away from

his sides. "How many times have I asked you not to call me that, Franky?"

Franky appeared to relax, but kept his gun trained at Johnson. "These guys with you, Moustache?"

Mustafa nodded. "Everything's cool."

Franky lowered his weapon and stepped up to Mustafa, clapping him in a hug. "They told me you'd gone off to see how security was managed on another colony. I didn't buy it." He held Mustafa at arms length. "So, what was it? Undercover work?"

Johnson coughed. "Aren't you going to introduce us?"

Franky let Mustafa go, and glanced at his men. He quickly waved their weapons down, then looked at Johnson.

Mustafa stepped forward. "Not here. Shall we go to the control room?"

Chapter 11

Seivers leant against a wall at the back of the control room, listening to the others talking quickly in hushed tones. It seemed that Mustafa and Frank had trained together on this mining colony. She looked up when a short, powerful man walked in.

Gotta be their boss.

"Glad to have you back, Chief." The man's voice was loud and hearty, and he reached his arms out to embrace Mustafa.

"And Centurion... Anson, wasn't it?" He punched Anson in the shoulder hard enough to knock him back a step, but his face showed no malice. "I had begun to think you would not be returning as promised."

Anson loosened his shoulders and held his arm out to Johnson. "Here is the leader I spoke of. Prefect Johnson speaks for the Legion and, in this matter, for Concorde."

The man bowed to Johnson. "Andrei Draxos, at your service. The news of the bombing of

Concorde reached us even here on Lavrio. I have to confess that I had my doubts about your centurion's words until that point."

"Very few believed our warnings," said Johnson. "The offer of an alliance still stands."

No-one who heard the warnings on Concorde believed them either.

"You know I cannot declare against Congress," said Draxos. "They would simply send in ships and replace my people."

"There would be no need for any such public declaration. As a Congressional world in a state of emergency, the Concorde government can place a priority claim on your resources. You can safely refuse any other requests while that claim is in place."

Draxos raised an eyebrow.

"But unlike your current clients, we intend to offer a fair exchange. Food, protection. A place in our alliance."

Draxos beamed. "Real meat?"

Ha! Got him.

"Well, in time, yes," said Johnson. "But to start with, just ration packs."

Mustafa rummaged in his pockets, and threw a ration bar at Draxos. "Their ration packs are still better than what we usually get."

Draxos took a bite and chewed thoughtfully. "Are you planning on actual physical protection, or just this legalese you mentioned?"

"The Concorde government is prepared to station a ship here. There will also, of course, be frequent visits from escorted freighters."

"What would you have us produce?"

"Officially, farm machinery, construction materials, parts for the terraforming plants," said Johnson.

"Unofficially?"

Here we go...

"Weapons, combat robots, ship armour."

Draxos blinked. "If we get caught building combat robots, a document from your government isn't going to save us."

Johnson smiled. "We'd be prepared to let you keep the first batch. Train you to use them to defend yourselves."

"I'm sure you could adapt the designs to make mining robots," added Anson. "They could considerably increase your production."

"If you'd give me a minute to confer with my people?" Draxos turned his back on Johnson and whispered with Mustafa and a couple of others.

The conversation became animated.

Mustafa isn't happy about something.

When Draxos turned back, he grinned and reached out both arms. "Prefect Johnson, I think we probably have a deal."

Seivers perked up at the word 'probably'. She glanced around the others in the room, noting that Anson had also stiffened.

"I'll leave you with Frank and Mustafa to iron out the kinks," said Draxos, before striding out of the room.

"What is it, Mustafa?" asked Anson.

Mustafa looked up. "I'm sorry. I didn't know about this."

I believe you.

Frank coughed. "Draxos would like you to demonstrate your commitment to our protection."

Anson stepped closer to the local, towering over him. "What sort of demonstration?"

Frank stood his ground. "Since Mustafa left, a warlord has moved into our system. He has set up a base on an asteroid. He demands we deliver him food and materiel."

"Couldn't you have asked one of the navy patrols to clear him out?" asked Anson.

Seivers wondered what was going through Johnson's mind, why she was letting Anson do the talking.

"We did mention it. They did nothing," replied Frank. "I suspected they were in his pocket, or the other way around. Or perhaps they figured we just weren't worth it."

Johnson turned to Seivers. "You up for a little pirate-hunting?"

Do you have to ask?

Seivers studied her nails. "Certainly beats all this talking."

#

A couple of days later, Razor-11 coasted towards the warlord's asteroid base. Running cold and dark it slipped past a patrolling ship.

"Quite hot for a little gang of pirates," said Seivers. "I count five patrols, and four more ships docked."

"They're mostly converted freighters and leisure craft." Johnson pointed at her terminal. "Apart from that one at the end of the space dock. That's a G-class corvette."

"How'd they get one of those?" called Mustafa

from the locker room.

Johnson glanced back. "Fleet sells off obsolete kit to… interested parties."

They drifted on for another few minutes.

"Whoa," said Johnson sitting upright.

Seivers looked across at her. "What?"

"The patrol pattern shifted."

Seivers squinted at the display screens in front of her. Nothing stood out.

"We got made. Hit it."

Seivers grinned. "Hell yeah!" She lifted the safety cover on a switch and flipped it. Power surged through Razor-11 as systems came back to life.

Johnson's fingers danced across her terminal and targeting data flooded onto Seivers' visor display. Racks popped out of the ship's sides and missiles streaked out.

"You strapped in back there?" Seivers shouted. An image of the two man in their armoured suits frantically trying to tie themselves down leapt into her mind.

"Have been since the Prefect got suspicious," said Anson through the comms, the model of calm.

Of course they were. Boring.

Seivers grabbed the throttle in her left hand and the stick with her right. "OK. Hold on."

She pushed the stick vertically downwards, barely resisting letting out a whoop as her stomach rose in her chest. A twist of the stick spun them sideways, then she slammed the throttle forwards.

Now it's my turn.

The acceleration piled weight onto her chest and she fought to keep her head straight against the seat. Her peripheral vision disappeared and she focussed on the narrowing window in front of her. Seivers gently tweaked the controls, beginning an arc that would bring them round to the side of the asteroid with the main base.

Three amber medical warnings flashed up in the centre of her HUD.

Dammit. Forgot they weren't pilots.

She gave it another second on then eased off a fraction. The alerts subsided to yellow.

Johnson groaned. "Haven't been that heavy since I flew shuttles. Was always jealous of fighter pilot physiology."

"Reverse burn'll be worse," said Seivers. She thought back to the days spent in gravity cells during training. The instructors had taken one look at her waiflike body and assumed she'd wash out. A quick calculation showed that the coming deceleration would be the harshest she'd experienced. Her parents hadn't intended her to use her adaptations in this way, but she thanked them anyway.

Johnson nodded. "Probably not worth reviving the other two until we're there."

A series of new stars burst into life as the missiles slammed home. One by one the hostile contacts vanished from the displays, replaced by navigation warnings for drifting debris.

"It's so clinical," said Seivers, juggling the joy of success with horror at the remote killing.

"Those converted craft were completely outclassed. Little in the way of modern countermeasures and virtually no armour," said Johnson. "When they get that corvette going we'll have a proper fight on our hands."

The asteroid loomed large in front of them. Seivers grimaced. "Let's not give it a chance, then."

She cut the mains, flipped Razor-11 end over end, and rammed the throttle forwards again. Once more the medical warnings lit on her HUD as she fought the elephant sitting on her chest.

Johnson's head snapped round as she passed out, her seat preventing injury. Seivers' skin crawled back across her face. Her vision narrowed to a tunnel. She concentrated on the readout showing distance to the asteroid, unable to see anything else.

OK. So in-head graphics would be pretty useful right now.

She experimented with the throttle, teasing every last bit of thrust without blacking out. After what felt like hours, but couldn't have been more than minutes, she killed the mains once more. In the delicious lightness of ballistic flight she deployed the ship's pulse cannons. Three bursts from the rear turrets were enough to shred the doors on the pirate base's landing bay. Seivers only had a moment to notice the lack of incoming fire as she manoeuvred through the gap, her final deceleration burn searing the inside of the bay.

That would never have worked against a military base. We're lucky they're didn't expect to be attacked.

Razor-11 came to a stop less than a metre from the back wall and settled onto its gear as if it was just returning from a simple patrol.

Seivers release the controls and let out a breath. "Piece of cake."

"Wha?" said Johnson, rubbing her neck.

"We're here, Ma'am," replied Seivers, pulling up all the external camera feeds on her displays. "Looks quiet for now, but something tells me they'll be along shortly to ask for a docking fee."

Chapter 12

Johnson released her restraints, the gel-filled chest piece swinging up over the seat's headrest. "You going to be OK?"

"I got it," said Seivers, dialling down the power on the pulse cannons. "If things get too hot here, I'll take off and find somewhere else to pick you up."

Johnson patted her on the shoulder and moved through to the locker room to find Mustafa and Anson fitting the helmets to their hardsuit armour.

"You sure you're OK in a firmsuit, Ma'am?" asked Anson, waving his bulk, angular arm across her rubbery attire.

"Those powered suits aren't flexible enough for my liking," replied Johnson, picking up her own helmet. "Besides, it's good to have options. We may need someone to fit though a small gap or something."

The three of them filed into the exit corridor and

Johnson sealed the hatch behind them. They all checked their weapons as the air cycled out, releasing the safeties and syncing their EIS feeds. Johnson opened two windows in her secondary consciousness, one with the feed from each of her companion's cameras.

Anson glanced back along the line then popped the bottom hatch. In rapid succession all three dropped to the ground and sprinted for the nearest exit to the landing bay, spreading out as they went. Johnson felt for a network connection but the frequencies were all empty.

Must've cooked the routers when we came in.

Anson was first to the door and pressed himself against the wall to its right. Mustafa hit the wall to the left as Anson stuck a charge to the lock. The moment Johnson took position behind him, he blew it. The metal door slammed open, propelled by the decompressing air behind it. Johnson felt the clang through the wall, relieved that Mustafa had taken position far enough away to avoid being hit.

The outgushing of air died quickly and the team moved into the airlock. Johnson pulled the door closed behind her and sealed it with a can of repair spray. The moment the airlock indicated it was airtight and released the interlock, Anson punched the open button. Mustafa crouched, training his rifle under the rising hatch. The door was halfway up when his rifle spoke twice. Anson ducked out into the workshop, firing three careful shots. Mustafa and Johnson followed. Movement on a walkway high and right caught Johnson's attention and she brought her pulse carbine up. Her first shot melted a hole in a metal support. Molten metal splattered on her metallo-ceramic chest and shoulder armour. Her second shot hit a pirate in the chest and took him down.

Johnson connected to the base network and launched a suite of hacking routines. Mustafa knelt behind a workbench, firing down a corridor whenever someone poked their head round the corner at the end. Johnson spotted something in his camera feed and she rewound it a few seconds. Playing it through again slowly in her secondary consciousness, she focused her primary consciousness on evaluating the exits. In her tertiary consciousness, she studied the results of the hacking routines. She saw what it was that had pulled her attention to Mustafa's feed and rolled to one side, riddling an air duct with holes until a body fell out.

^I've jammed their comms,^ she sent via EIS. ^Not got into their storage system yet.^

^We can't hold here any longer,^ sent Anson.

^Agreed,^ sent Johnson, setting a new routine to specifically hunt out a floor plan. ^Take this corridor in three.^

She tagged the corridor on the team map and started a countdown. On zero, they all rose and plastered the enemy positions with fire. A micromissile from Anson's backpack whined down the corridor ahead of them and exploded at the next junction.

^Keep moving. Right here,^ she sent. ^Without comms they can't coordinate and block us.^

A floorplan opened in her tertiary consciousness. She studied it as she ran, telling a routine to convert the file and include it in the team map.

^This is the first place we look,^ she sent, marking a room in a red glow. ^I reckon it's the command centre.^

They met little resistance for the next few hundred metres. Data started to flood into Johnson's mind as her hacking routines won out against the base network's defences. ^They were paid by Fleet to set up here. Downloading their accounts now.^

Mustafa sent the impression of a bad smell. ^Figures. Always trying to keep the miners down.^

^Seems our target's name is Xander.^ Johnson relaxed a tiny fraction. ^OK. I'm into their control systems. Locking down all hatches. Patching into internal sensors. Identifying personnel... Got him!^

The positions of all the defenders populated the map, one of them marked with a crown. The team set off at a gentle lope. Johnson opened and closed the hatches as they went, picking an unopposed route. She pulled up the feed from the room in which the warlord was trapped. Sumptuous red and gold drapes hid the bare metal of the walls, a large bed the centrepiece of the room. The target himself wore an armoured vest and held a thermal shotgun. He crouched behind the bed, eyes fixed on the door.

Anson arrived at the bedroom door first. He leant beside it whilst Mustafa covered him from across the corridor. Anson looked at Johnson and pointed at the access panel. She nodded and held a hand up for him to wait.

Johnson connected to the room's comm panel.

"Congressional Navy. Lay down your weapon and surrender."

"No you're not," Xander shouted back.

Johnson displayed her credentials on the screen. "I assure you we are. And you are under arrest."

The warlord sat back against the bed, tension draining from his face. "Wait until Commodore Naidu hears about this. I'll be out and you'll be in a whole heap of trouble."

It was Johnson's turn to smile. "He's not in my chain of command. I report directly to the government of Concorde, acting under emergency powers."

Xander stiffened and trained his shotgun back on the door.

^You should have left him believing we were locals,^ sent Mustafa. ^He might have given up easy.^

Johnson cursed internally. "In case you hadn't realised, I have complete control of your base's systems. Surrender or I pump the air out of your room until you pass out. Either way I'm arresting you."

The warlord shifted his weight. Johnson's tertiary consciousness noticed some of the warlord's men had found cutting equipment and were making their way towards them. She cut the lights and the fans supplying air to the warlord's chamber.

"OK, OK," he shouted. The shotgun clattered to the floor.

Johnson set a three second timer on the team's vision. On zero she unlocked the door and cut the corridor lights. Anson pushed the door open with one arm. Mustafa stepped quickly inside, sweeping his weapon around. Anson followed. Johnson kept her weapon pointed at the doorway, her secondary consciousness watching through Mustafa's camera as Anson approached the warlord. His limbs and face glowed bright in infra-red as he knelt on the floor.

^We gotta move,^ Johnson sent. ^They're almost here.^

^Coming out,^ replied Anson seconds later.

Mustafa emerged first. The warlord followed, hands cuffed behind him, no longer wearing armour. Anson walked several paces further back, stun pistol pointed at his back.

Johnson guided them back to the workshop where they'd entered the base. Mustafa found an emergency space suit and helped Xander don it, freeing his hands. Anson sent a puzzled question mark.

^He'll need them for the ladder,^ Mustafa replied.

They entered a working airlock and cycled it.

"We're coming out of airlock orange three," Johnson radioed to Razor-11.

"Clear to approach," replied Seivers. "Just make it quick before they come back again."

The hatch opened and they sprinted for their ship. Charred bodies littered the hanger, clustered mostly around the airlocks. They slid to a halt under Razor-11 and trained their weapons back the way they'd come. As the ladder descended, bright blue flashes silently filled the hanger.

^You first,^ sent Anson.

Johnson scurried up the ladder, Razor-11's pulse cannons continuing to light up the space around her. Once inside she slung her carbine round to her back and drew her stun pistol.

Seconds later Xander's head emerged and she trained her weapon on him. "Easy now."

She backed up to the inner hatch as Mustafa clambered up into the chamber. Anson had just got his upper body inside when the ship jerked upward. Mustafa moved to grab him but Anson shook his head and rolled up onto the floor. Johnson triggered the hatch to close.

"Can't hang around," said Seivers.

Johnson and Mustafa dragged the warlord into the locker room and strapped him in to a seat. They cuffed his ankles and wrists to the seat, leaving his helmet locked in case of a hull breach. Anson and Mustafa sat and engaged their restraints while Johnson scrabbled through to the cockpit. The moment she sat, Seivers thrust forwards. Johnson's restraint swung down into place and she logged in to the tactical terminal.

"Looks like they've got the corvette going," Johnson said. "Standing by on countermeasures."

Seivers steered for open space. "Shame we don't have any more missiles. Make them think twice before following us."

"Hopefully they don't know that." Johnson dug through the data she'd mined from the base's network and opened a channel direct to the corvette. "Stand down or we will be forced to engage you."

After a brief pause a gruff voice replied. "You have offended us. You will not escape."

The corvette powered up its mains.

"We have your lord," said Johnson. "If you fire on us, you risk killing him."

"Hah! He let himself be captured. He is no longer our lord."

Three missiles leapt from the corvette and arced to close on Razor-11 from different directions.

"So be it." Johnson cut the connection and released a spread of countermeasure pods. These confused two of the missiles, allowing a pulse cannon to take out the third.

The clang of a railgun round hitting the hull sent the ship into a spin, which Seivers exaggerated to get them out of the stream of metal. For a moment they were flying backwards, and Seivers sent a trio of shots from their own axial railgun back at the corvette. One hit.

Five more missiles rippled out of the larger ship, all heading straight for them. Johnson popped more countermeasures and the pulse cannons sung. When the interference from exploding warheads cleared, Johnson blinked in disbelief. "She's turning."

"Did I do some damage with the railgun?" asked Seivers.

Johnson shook her head. "Nothing that would put them out of the fight... Looks like they're making a run for the gamma jump point."

Seivers altered course for the mining colony. Johnson switched to a strategic display. "Ah!"

"What?" asked Seivers.

"*Tigre* and another frigate just jumped in," replied Johnson. "Well, their light arrived a minute ago anyway."

"They're, what, twenty light-minutes out?" said Seivers, switching to autopilot but keeping her hands near the manual controls.

"Eighteen. The pirates might just make it before they can intercept." Johnson parcelled the data they'd collected and transmitted it to the frigates, along with an order for one to pursue the corvette as far as the jump point.

"Should I stand down from general quarters?" asked Seivers

Johnson thought for a moment. "Give it another ten minutes. No point relaxing too soon, they may yet have a trick for us."

Chapter 13

"I'll miss the excuse to come down here," said Johnson, reclining in a canvas chair in the small hangar where she'd rebuilt Razor-11.

Seivers sipped from her bottle of beer, trying to work out what it was about the prefect that made her trust her. The loose-fitting sweatshirt certainly made her look less threatening, but it was more than that. Something behind her eyes.

"But she's yours now." Johnson raised her bottle.

Seivers raised her own bottle in reply. "You're welcome to drop by and tinker."

Johnson nodded, and fell silent for a few moments.

"It seems that an AI has volunteered to work with you," said Johnson. "It isn't a full sentience like Indie or Orion, but it has already developed a unique identity."

Seivers cocked her head to one side.

"It prefers to talk to people," Johnson explained. "It had to be isolated from its peers because it became convinced they were deliberately ganging up on it."

Seivers snorted. "Can it fly?"

"It has over a thousand hours in simulations," replied Johnson. "That's real-time hours; subjectively we're talking years."

Seivers rolled the collar of her turquoise jumper. "And you want me to teach it flair."

Johnson nodded.

"OK," said Seivers with a sigh. "What do I have to do?"

"Nothing." Johnson paused. "There, the transfer has begun."

"What is this AI like?" asked Seivers?

Johnson shrugged. "Why don't you go and find out for yourself. The transfer will have finished by you get to the flight deck."

Seivers took a last swig from her bottle and rose decisively. She climbed the ladder, and made her way to the front. Sitting in her chair, she looked around hesitantly.

"Hello?" she called.

A male voice came through the speakers, echoing as if coming from far side of a large room. "Hello yourself."

Seivers shook her head, her azure hair flicking

to one side. "I'm Anastasia Seivers. I understand that you volunteered to work with me?"

"Ah, right." The voice sounded closer. "I am Percy."

Seivers covered her laugh with a cough.

"Are you choking?"

"No," she replied, fanning herself with her hand. "Sorry. I had expected something a little grander."

"My full name is *The Perception of Prejudice*. But that is a bit pretentious, do you not think?"

-o-

Equality

The fruity stench of manure filled the hold of the freighter. A middle-aged man crouched in the corner, holding his wife and young son as the ship bucked and jolted. The lights flickered and went out.

"Ssshhh, ssshhhh. It'll be all right. We're just entering the atmosphere."

The ship dropped for several seconds, leaving the man's stomach high in his chest, and the boy cried out. His mother stroked his hair and glared at her husband.

He looked away. It was his fault they were riding in such atrocious conditions. They had the money to travel in style, but he didn't want to draw attention to their passage. One day he'd be able to explain it to her, some of it anyway.

The buffeting eased and the main lights came back on. Two of his assistants rose and checked the animals. The tranquilisers had saved the beasts the stress of the descent, but they weren't without risk. He knew he should go help them, but couldn't bring himself to let go of his son.

#

The *Two Democracies: Revolution* series will continue with *Equality*.

If you want progress updates and an alert when any other books by Alasdair Shaw are published, please join my mailing list:

http://www.alasdairshaw.co.uk/newsletter/perception.php

You can also follow *The Indescribable Joy of Destruction* on Twitter: https://twitter.com/IndieAI and on Facebook:
https://www.facebook.com/twodemocracies.

If you particularly enjoyed it, I'd greatly appreciate a share on Facebook or a Tweet.

Also by Alasdair Shaw

Two Democracies: Revolution

Repulse – a 2500 word short story (in The Newcomer anthology)
Independence – a 6,000 word short story
Liberty – a 105,000 word novel
The Perception of Prejudice – a 14,000 word novelette
Equality – a novel (planned for summer 2017)
Fraternity – a novel
Unity – a novel